D0689726

If Wendell Had a Walrus

Lori Mortensen

illustrated by Matt Phelan

Henry Holt and Company
New York

Henry Holt and Company, *Publishers since 1866*
Henry Holt® is a registered trademark of Macmillan Publishing Group, LLC
175 Fifth Avenue, New York, New York 10010 • mackids.com

Library of Congress Cataloging-in-Publication Data
Names: Mortensen, Lori, 1955– author. | Phelan, Matt, illustrator.
Title: If Wendell had a walrus / Lori Mortensen ; illustrated by Matt Phelan.
Description: First edition. | New York : Henry Holt and Company, 2018.
Summary: Wendell gœs looking for a walrus but finds a new friend instead.
Identifiers: LCCN 2017004846 | ISBN 978-1-62779-602-6 (hardcover)
Subjects: | CYAC: Friendship—Fiction.
Classification: LCC PZ7.M84643 If 2018 | DDC [E]—dc23
LC record available at https://lccn.loc.gov/2017004846

First edition, 2018 / Designed by April Ward
The artist used pencil and watercolor to create the illustrations for this book.
Printed in China by RR Donnelley Asia Printing Solutions Ltd., Dongguan City, Guangdong Province
1 3 5 7 9 10 8 6 4 2

To my daydreaming dad, Wendell,
and his brother, Morrell
—L. M.

To Robert, Bill, and Marc
—M. P.

One day, Wendell was minding his own business when a walrus floated by.

Of course, it wasn't a **real** walrus. Just a cloud one.

But when Wendell saw it, he started thinking about **real** ones all the same.

If Wendell had a walrus, he'd name him Roger.

They'd tell tons of jokes. Walruses love a good joke.

Then they'd jump on Wendell's bike and pedal right past old Mrs. Quimby's house. Wouldn't **she** be surprised!

They'd climb trees,
You can do it!
build forts,
Our fort doesn't need a roof!

fly kites,

draw ducks
and maybe a dinghy,

and have the most
stupendiferous,
cosmically colossal
best time of their lives.

If Wendell had a walrus.

But he didn't.

Not one.

As he sat on a rock, he came up with the best idea ever. Why didn't he think of it before?

Wendell marched down to
Uncle Zed's Pet Emporium.

"I'll have one walrus, please."

"Sorry," said Uncle Zed. Unfortunately, he didn't expect a walrus shipment in the foreseeable future.

Wendell thought and thought.

"Of course!" he said. It was best to ask a walrus directly.

Wendell wrote a note, stuffed it in a bottle, and tossed it into the ocean.

Dear Mr. Walrus,
How are you? If you're tired of your iceberg, come on over to my house. Here's a map.
Hope to see you soon.

Yours truly,
Wendell

BIG tree
you
me

As it floated away, Wendell couldn't help noticing another boy with another bottle.

"Walrus?" asked Wendell.

"Whale," said the boy.

Now all they had to do was wait.

And wait.

And wait.

Since waiting was rather tiresome, Wendell and the boy, who was named Morrell, decided to pass the time together . . .

telling jokes,

riding bikes,

climbing trees,
Have you ever climbed this high before?
building forts,
Fort Mordell!

flying kites,

drawing ducks

and maybe some dinghies,

and having the most
stupendiferous,
cosmically colossal
best time of their lives.

When would Wendell get a walrus?

There was no rush.

You got one, too?